The Reading Race

Ready, Freddy!

Ready, Freddy!

The Reading Race

by ABBY KLEIN

illustrated by
JOHN McKINLEY

Scholastic Inc.

To Donna Sullivan-MacDonald and Judy Gilmartin,
Thank you for inspiring so many young readers each
and every day with your passion for reading and your
love of books!

No part of this publication may be reproduced, stored in a retrieval
system, or transmitted in any form or by any means, electronic,
mechanical, photocopying, recording, or otherwise, without written
permission of the publisher. For information regarding permission,
write to Scholastic Inc., Attention: Permissions Department,
557 Broadway, New York, NY 10012.

ISBN 978-0-545-55044-4

Text copyright © 2013 by Abby Klein
Illustrations copyright © 2013 by John McKinley
All rights reserved. Published by Scholastic Inc.
SCHOLASTIC and associated logos are trademarks
and/or registered trademarks of Scholastic Inc.

12 11 10 9 8 7 6 5 4 3 2 1   13 14 15 16 17 18/0

Printed in the U.S.A.   40

First printing, September 2013

CHAPTERS

I have a problem.

A really, really big problem.

My school is having a book fair. The week before the fair we are having a Read-a-thon, and the person who reads for the most minutes gets to choose five free books at the book fair! I really want to win the books, but I'm not a very good reader.

Let me tell you about it.

CHAPTER 1

The Read-A-Thon

"Come sit on the rug, everybody," said our teacher, Mrs. Wushy. "I have something exciting to tell you about."

We all walked over to the rug and sat down.

"Are we going on a field trip?" asked Robbie.

"No," said Mrs. Wushy.

"I know! I know!" Chloe yelled. "We're going to have a party. I just love parties!"

"No, not a party," said Mrs. Wushy. "Maybe this will give you a clue." She reached over, picked up a stack of papers, and handed one to each of us.

"The book fair!" we all said together. "The book fair is coming!"

Max jumped up off the rug and started bouncing up and down. "Oh yeah! Oh yeah! Oh yeah!" he sang as he pumped his fist in the air. By accident, he stepped on Chloe's finger.

"Owww, owww, owww!" she screamed. She was running around and shaking her finger in the air. "You broke my finger! You broke my finger!"

"I did not!" yelled Max.

"Yes, you did!" Chloe cried.

"Did not!"

"Did too!"

"All right. That's enough," said Mrs. Wushy. "Chloe, let me see your finger."

Chloe held out her finger so Mrs. Wushy could look at it. "See. It's broken. I can only move it this much."

"If it were broken, she wouldn't be able to move it at all," my best friend, Robbie, whispered to me.

"She is such a drama queen," said Jessie.

Mrs. Wushy gently touched Chloe's finger. "I don't think it's broken."

"I told you," said Max.

"Well, it's all red," said Chloe. "Look." She waved her finger in Max's face.

"I wouldn't do that if I were her," said Robbie.

"Yeah," I said. "Last time she did that, he bit her finger!"

Jessie giggled. "Just like an angry dog."

Max took a step toward Chloe.

"Watch out!" Robbie whispered.

Mrs. Wushy put her hand on Max's shoulder. "You need to apologize to Chloe."

"Why?" said Max. "If she had her hands in her lap, then I wouldn't have stepped on her finger."

"No," said Mrs. Wushy. "If you were sitting

11

quietly on the rug instead of jumping up and down, then this wouldn't have happened. You really need to be more careful."

"Yeah, Max," said Chloe. "You need to calm down."

"Max, we're waiting," said Mrs. Wushy.

"For what?"

"For you to say you're sorry."

Max sighed. "Fine, I'm sorry," he mumbled.

"What?" said Chloe. "I didn't hear you."

"I'm sorry!" he yelled in her face.

"Max, that was not very kind. Please tell Chloe you're sorry in a nice voice."

"I'm sorry," he said again.

"Much better," said Mrs. Wushy. "Now please go sit in that chair."

Max went to sit in a chair by the edge of the rug.

"Chloe, why don't you go over to the sink and run your finger under some cold water? That will make it feel a lot better."

"I think I need to go to the nurse," said Chloe.

"Go to the nurse?" I whispered to Robbie. "She's acting like she got her finger cut off."

Robbie giggled.

"No," said Mrs. Wushy. "I think your finger will be fine if you just put some cold water on it."

Chloe walked over to the sink, and Mrs. Wushy came back to the front of the class. "Now, where was I?" she said.

"You were telling us about the book fair," said Robbie.

"That's right," said Mrs. Wushy. "The book fair will be here next week."

"I can't wait!" I said. "I just love the book fair."

"Me, too," said Jessie. "There are always so many cool books."

"Like this one," said Robbie, pointing to a book on the paper Mrs. Wushy had given us. "It's called *The Night I Saved the Universe*. It's about a boy who goes into outer space with an alien police officer to help him solve crimes."

"Are there any Angelina Ballerina books?" Chloe asked as she walked back to the rug. "Those are my favorite. Angelina is a ballerina just like me." She spun around once before she sat down.

"Oh, look," said Jessie. "Here's a cool book about basketball. I'm going to ask my *abuela*, my grandma, if I can get this one."

"Girls can't buy basketball books," said Max.

"Why not?" asked Jessie.

"Because those are boy books," said Max.

"There is no such thing as boy books and girl books," said Jessie. "Boys and girls can read any books they want."

"That's right," said Mrs. Wushy. "And I need all of the boys and all of the girls to do a lot of reading in the next week."

"Why?" asked Robbie.

"Because the book fair is holding a contest," said Mrs. Wushy.

"A contest?" said Max. "What kind of contest?"

"Well," said Mrs. Wushy, "we're going to have a Read-a-thon for one week, and the person who reads for the most minutes will get to pick five free books from the book fair."

"Five free books! Wow!" said Max. "That's awesome!"

"There's more," said Mrs. Wushy.

"More?" said Robbie. "Really?"

"Really," said Mrs. Wushy. "Each class will add

up all their reading minutes, and the class that has the highest total will get an author visit."

"No way!" said Robbie. "I've always wanted to meet a real live author."

Mrs. Wushy gave us each another piece of paper. "So here is the paper you need to fill out each day with your number of reading minutes. Your parents also have to sign it."

"That's so you don't cheat," Chloe said, looking at Max.

"I'm not a cheater. You are!" Max said to Chloe.

"I am not!" Chloe whined.

"Oh boy, here we go again," I said.

"You two need to stop," said Mrs. Wushy. "It is not polite to call someone a cheater, and no one in our class cheats."

Chloe and Max glared at each other.

Mrs. Wushy continued, "So for the next week, let's all read, read, read. I bet if we all work really hard, we can win that author visit."

CHAPTER 2

Let Me Tell!

That night when it was time for dessert, my dad asked, "Did anything happen at school today?"

"Yes! Do you want to hear something cool?" I said.

"He was talking to me, Hammerhead," said Suzie. "Not you."

"How do you know?" I said.

"Because he was looking at me," said Suzie.

"So?"

"So, that means he was asking *me*."

"That's okay," said my dad. "You can both tell me something. Suzie, why don't you go first?"

Suzie smiled at me and then turned to my dad and said, "The book fair is coming next week, and —"

"And there's going to be a contest!" I interrupted.

"That's not fair!" Suzie whined. "I was going to say that. Freddy ruined it!"

"You can still tell us about it," said my mom.

"No, I can't," Suzie said, pouting. "He already told you."

"I'd like to hear more about the contest," said my dad. "So if you're not going to tell me, then Freddy can. Freddy, do you want to tell me about it?"

"Sure, Dad. There's going to be a Read-a-thon for a whole week. We're all supposed to keep track of how many minutes we read each day —"

"And the person who reads the most minutes gets to pick five free books from the book fair," said Suzie.

"Hey, I was telling them," I said, "and you interrupted."

"Now you know how it feels," said Suzie.

I stuck my tongue out at her.

"Freddy, do not stick your tongue out at your sister. That's rude," said my dad.

"Well, she was rude to me," I said.

"If you two don't stop arguing, there will be no dessert," said my mom.

"No dessert! But you got my favorite ice cream, mint chocolate chip, at the grocery store today and told me I could have some for dessert," I said.

"Then you will stop fighting with your sister," said my mom.

"But what about *her*?"

"She needs to stop, too." My mom looked at both of us.

We glared at each other.

"I guess I can put this ice cream back in the freezer," said my mom.

I had been waiting all day for that ice cream.

"No, wait!" Suzie and I said together. "We'll be good."

"Promise?" said my mom.

"Promise," we said.

My mom scooped out the ice cream and passed a bowl to each of us. I stuck my head in my bowl to smell it. "Mmmmm, I just love the fresh, minty smell."

When I lifted my head up, Suzie started pointing and laughing at me.

"What's so funny?" I said.

"You . . . you . . . you have ice cream on your nose."

I looked carefully at the tip of my nose. Sure enough, it was green. I tried to lick it off with my tongue.

"Freddy, what are you doing?" said my mom.

"Trying to get the ice cream off the end of my nose," I said.

"How about using a napkin instead of your tongue?"

"But my way is more fun," I said.

"Your way is disgusting," said my mom.

"But, look. I almost got it all off," I said, sticking my tongue way out of my mouth and tickling the end of my nose.

"Freddy, please use your napkin."

"Oh, all right," I said. I picked up my napkin and wiped off the end of my nose. "Mom, do we have any chocolate syrup?"

"Yes, it's on the bottom shelf of the fridge."

I went over to the refrigerator and grabbed the bottle of chocolate syrup. I brought it back to the table and poured it over my ice cream.

"Whoa, whoa, whoa," said my dad. "I think that's enough, Freddy."

"You can never have enough chocolate," I said, smiling. I stuck my finger in the chocolate syrup and then rubbed it on my top lip. "Look, I have a chocolate mustache!"

"Freddy," said my mom, "you have to stop playing with your food. You are not a baby anymore."

"Sometimes I wonder," Suzie mumbled to herself.

"Go over to the sink and wash off your face and hands right now. And don't touch anything on your way over."

"It's just a little chocolate syrup," I said.

"And a little chocolate syrup can make a big mess," my mom said. She is such a Neat Freak that she thinks everything is a big mess.

I washed up and came back to the table to finish my dessert.

"Here's a spoon," said my mom. "Use it, or I'll have to start calling you Little Piggy."

"So, can we finish talking about the book fair?" said my dad. "Did you say that the person who reads the most minutes gets five free books?"

"Five free books of your choice," said Suzie.

"Isn't that cool?" I said. "You get to pick them yourself."

"That is pretty cool," said my dad.

"What a great contest," said my mom. "Of course, I like anything that gets you to read."

"I think I'm going to win," said Suzie. "I love to read."

"How about you, Freddy?" said my mom.

"I really want those books, but I can't win," I said. "I am not a very good reader."

"Yes, you are," said my dad.

"No, I'm not," I said. "And besides, Suzie can read much faster than I can."

"So?" said my dad.

"So, there's no way I can read that fast."

"Remember," said my mom. "You're not counting how many books you read. You're counting the minutes. You don't need to read more books than Suzie. You just need to read for more minutes than she does."

I sat up in my chair and smiled. "Hey, you're right, Mom. Why didn't I think of that?"

I gobbled the rest of my ice cream and jumped out of my chair.

"Where are you going?" my mom asked.

"Where do you think?" I said. "To read!"

"No Commander Upchuck tonight?" said my dad.

"Nope," I said. "No time for TV. I've got to read, read, read!"

CHAPTER 3

All Night Long

I ran upstairs to my room and started pulling books off my bookshelf, looking for my favorite shark book.

"No, not this one," I said as I tossed a book on the floor. "Not this one, or this one, or this one." Each time, I looked at the title and then tossed it aside.

I had pulled twenty more books off the shelf and still hadn't found my favorite one when Suzie walked in the room.

"Get out of here!" I yelled. "What are you doing?"

"What are *you* doing?" she said. "Look at this pile of books. You are going to be in so much trouble when Mom finds out about this mess."

"I'll clean it up as soon as I find the book I'm looking for."

"Which one are you looking for?"

"Don't Eat the Teacher."

"Why do you need it so badly?" Suzie said.

"Because I know that one by heart. It's easy for me to read, so I want to read it tonight. Do you know where it is?"

"Maybe."

"What do you mean 'maybe'?"

"Maybe I know where it is."

"So tell me where it is," I said.

"I don't know for sure," said Suzie.

"What do you mean you don't know for sure? You just told me you knew where it was."

"When you asked me where it was, I said maybe I knew where it was," said Suzie. "Maybe."

"AARRGGHHH!" I growled. "Okay, then where do you *think* it is?"

"In the bathroom."

"The bathroom? Why is it in the bathroom?"

"I don't know, Stinkyhead!" said Suzie. "Maybe because you took it in there this morning."

"I did?"

"Yes, you did. I think you were going to take it to school, so you brought it in there when you were brushing your teeth, but then you forgot to take it."

"Oh yeah. I think you're right," I said.

"Of course I'm right," Suzie said, smiling. "I'm always right."

I ran past Suzie and pushed open the bathroom door. There it was. Sitting on the edge of the sink. Right where I left it. I picked it up and brought it back into my room. "Got it!" I said to Suzie. "Thanks."

"You're welcome. If I were you," Suzie said, "I'd get this mess cleaned up before Mom comes upstairs."

"Yeah, yeah," I mumbled. "Do you want to help me?"

"Nope," said Suzie, turning to walk out of my room. "I've got to start reading if I want to win this contest."

Great, just great, I thought to myself. *She's*

already going to be ahead of me. I stuck the books back on my shelf as quickly as possible. I didn't want to lose any more reading time.

I sat down on my bed and began to read. I didn't realize how much time had passed until my mom came into my room. "Okay, honey. It's time for bed."

"What?"

"Freddy, it's time for bed," said my mom, "and you're not even in your pajamas yet."

"Sorry, Mom. I was reading."

"I really like hearing you say that," my mom said, "but now you need to put the book down and get ready for bed. It's late."

"But, Mom —"

"No buts. Go brush your teeth and put on your pajamas."

"Okay, okay," I said. I walked into the bathroom.

A few minutes later my mom came in. I was sitting on the toilet reading my book. "Freddy,

what are you doing?" said my mom. "I told you to get ready for bed."

"I just wanted to finish this book."

"Well, you can finish it in the morning. Right now it's bedtime. In fact, it's past your bedtime. You need to get to sleep. You have school tomorrow. You have five minutes to finish up and get in bed."

I rushed to brush my teeth and put on my pajamas in two minutes, so I could have three extra minutes to read my book in bed.

"Now you look ready, Freddy," said my mom when she walked into my room. "You'll have plenty of time to finish that book tomorrow."

"Good night, Mom," I said.

"Good night, Freddy," she said, giving me a kiss on the cheek. "Go to sleep." She turned off my light and closed the door.

As soon as I heard her footsteps disappear down the hall, I pulled my sharkhead flashlight out from under my covers.

Pretty sneaky, I thought to myself. *Now I can keep reading and she'll never know.*

I had only read one page when all of a sudden I heard my doorknob turning. My heart skipped a beat and I quickly shoved my flashlight and book under my covers.

"Hey, Freddy," said my dad, opening my bedroom door. "I didn't get to kiss you good night."

He walked over to my bed and sat down to give me a hug. He happened to sit right on the flashlight.

I gulped.

He pulled the flashlight out from under the covers. "What's this doing here?"

"I, uh . . . I, uh . . . I keep it there so the Dream Police can use it at night to scare away bad guys," I said.

My dad smiled. "Good idea," he said.

I breathed a sigh of relief. Whew, that was a close one.

"Well, good night. Sleep tight. Don't let the bad guys bite," said my dad, giving me a hug and a kiss.

"Good night, Dad," I said.

He left my room and closed the door. This time I waited until I heard his bedroom door close before I pulled the flashlight out again.

If I was going to win this contest, then I was going to have to read all night long.

CHAPTER 4

Too Tired

I must have fallen asleep sometime during the night, because the next thing I knew, Suzie was shaking me.

"Freddy, Freddy, wake up! Wake up!"

"Huh? What?" I mumbled.

"Wake up! You're late," said Suzie.

I was so tired I couldn't even open my eyes.

"What's your problem?" asked Suzie.

I didn't answer her.

"You need to get out of bed now. Mom sent me in here to get you up."

"Leave me alone," I said. I rolled over and put my pillow over my head. That was a mistake, because Suzie found the flashlight and the book.

"What's this?" she said, pulling the pillow off my head.

"What's what?"

"This," she said, holding the flashlight up to my nose.

"What does it look like?" I said. "Duh, it's a flashlight."

"I know it's a flashlight," said Suzie. "But why do you have it in your bed?"

I didn't answer.

She asked again. "Why do you have it in your bed?"

"None of your business."

"Well, it can be Mom's business. Maybe I'll go tell her."

"No! Wait!" I called. "You can't tell Mom."

"Then tell me why it's in your bed."

"I . . . I . . ."

"Spit it out, Sharkbreath. I don't have all morning."

"I was using it to read last night."

"Last night? You mean after lights-out?" Suzie said.

I nodded.

"Ooohhhhh, you are going to be in so much trouble."

"I was reading for the Read-a-thon so I could get lots of reading minutes. Please don't tell Mom and Dad," I said.

"What's it worth to you?" said Suzie.

"I'll make your bed tomorrow morning."

"Just tomorrow morning? You're crazy," said Suzie. "You make my bed for three days, and we have a deal."

"Three days! That's not fair," I said.

"Take it or leave it." Suzie stuck her pinkie out for a pinkie swear. That's how we sealed all our deals.

"Fine, pinkie swear," I said as we locked our pinkies together. "Now you can't tell them anything."

"You can't, either," Suzie said, smiling.

"What do you mean?" I said.

"You can't tell them you were up half the night reading because you'll get in trouble, so those minutes don't count. Remember, you have to have your parents sign the paper."

"UUUGGGHHH!" Why didn't I think of that? My brain was just too tired to think.

"So you stayed up half the night for nothing," said Suzie.

Just then we heard my mom calling, "Freddy, Suzie, where are you? It's getting late. You need to get down here now!"

Suzie ran downstairs to get breakfast.

I was not going to be able to do any running today. I was so tired, and now those minutes wouldn't even count!

I slowly got up out of bed, got dressed, and dragged myself downstairs.

"Well, look who's here," said my dad.

"Oh, Freddy!" said my mom. "Look at you!"

Suzie was giggling.

"What?" I said.

"Did you get dressed in the dark this morning?" said my dad.

Suzie kept laughing and pointing.

"What's so funny?" I said.

"Your shirt is on backwards. You have on two different colored socks, and you look like you had your hair done at the monster beauty parlor," said Suzie.

"Did you even brush your teeth and comb your hair this morning?" my mom asked.

"I think I forgot," I said, yawning.

"Why are you so tired?" said my dad.

"I didn't get much sleep last night."

"Why not?"

"I, uh . . . I, uh . . . ," I stammered.

"Go on. Tell them," Suzie said.

I glared at her.

"Were you on Monster Patrol? Helping out the Dream Police?" said my dad.

"Yeah, yeah, Monster Patrol," I said.

"Good thing you had that flashlight," said my dad.

"Uh-huh. Good thing," I said, looking over at Suzie and smiling.

"Why don't you eat your breakfast," said my mom, "and then you can go back upstairs and brush your teeth and comb your hair."

"Yeah, you wouldn't want to scare anyone at school with that shark breath and monster hairdo," said Suzie.

"Can I have pancakes today, Mom?" I asked.

"I don't think you have time for that," my mom said. She put a bowl of oatmeal down in front of me. "Here, eat this quickly. The bus is going to be here soon."

I started to eat my oatmeal, but I was so tired that my eyes began to close, and then my head fell forward right into my bowl.

"Oh my goodness!" yelled my mom. "Freddy! Freddy! Are you all right?"

"Ha, ha, ha!" Suzie laughed.

I lifted my head out of the bowl. My whole face was covered in oatmeal, and it was slowly sliding onto my pants.

My mom ran over with a towel to wipe me off. "Freddy, you just fell asleep in your oatmeal. Now it's dripping all over. What a mess!"

"Sorry, Mom. I'm just really tired."

"Now you need to go upstairs and wash up

and change before the bus gets here. You only have ten minutes. Hurry!"

"And make sure you put your shirt on the right way this time!" Suzie yelled after me. "I don't want to get on the bus with you looking like a dork!"

CHAPTER 5

Big-Mouth Bully

I just barely made it to the bus on time. I sat down next to Robbie.

"Boy, you don't look so good," said Robbie. "What's up?"

"Don't ask," I said. "Long story."

"We have a long bus ride, so you have time to tell me."

"Well," I said, "I was trying to read for a lot of minutes for the Read-a-thon, so I stayed up late."

"Your parents let you do that?"

"Not really," I said. "I waited until they had gone into their room, and then I got out my flashlight and read under my covers."

"Oh, that's a good idea," said Robbie.

"I thought so, too, until Suzie reminded me that my parents have to sign the paper telling how many minutes we've read. My mom and dad would be mad if they knew I was up past my bedtime reading. Now I'm super tired, and I can't count those minutes!"

"Bummer," said Robbie.

"Yeah," I said. "Huge bummer."

"Hey, stay still a minute," said Robbie. "You've got something in your hair." He pulled a chunk of dried oatmeal out of my hair. "What's this?"

"Oatmeal."

"Oatmeal?" said Robbie. "Ewwww. How did you get oatmeal in your hair?"

"I was so tired this morning that I fell asleep in my oatmeal."

"Ha, ha, ha!" said Max. "That is hilarious! I wish I had been there to see that!"

"Why does he always have to listen to our conversations?" I whispered to Robbie.

"Hey, everybody," said Max. "Listen to this. Freddy fell asleep in his oatmeal this morning."

The whole bus started laughing. I slid down in my seat.

"I can't believe he just announced it to the whole bus. Now everyone will think I'm a loser."

"Just ignore him," said Robbie.

"Yeah, I don't think you're a loser," said Jessie.

"Thanks, Jessie," I said. "How many minutes did you read last night?"

"I read for forty-five minutes," Chloe chirped.

"He wasn't asking you, Fancypants," said Max.

"Yes, he was," she said.

"Oh no, he wasn't," said Max.

"Then who was he talking to?" Chloe said leaning over her seat.

"He was asking Jessie," said Max. "No one was talking to you. No one cares how many minutes you read last night."

"You're just jealous," said Chloe. "How many minutes did you read last night? I bet you didn't even read for ten."

Max didn't answer.

"You're not as good a reader as I am," said Chloe. "I am the best reader in the class."

"That's not true," Max said.

"Yes, it is," said Chloe. "My mom always tells me that I am a super reader. She calls me the princess of reading. Do you know that I can read third-grade books all by myself?"

"So?" said Max.

"So, I bet you can't do that."

"Robbie can," I said. "Robbie can actually read fourth-grade books."

"Fourth grade?" said Chloe. "I don't believe it."

"Well, believe it," I said. "He is the king of reading!"

Chloe sat back down in her seat.

"Nice work," said Jessie. "Maybe that will keep her quiet for a while."

"So, how many minutes did you read for last night?" I said to Jessie.

"I read for sixty minutes."

"Wow! You read for a whole hour?"

"Yep," said Jessie.

"Good for you!" said Robbie.

"An hour is a long time," I said. "I don't think I could read for that long."

"My *abuela* had a really good idea," said Jessie. "She told me that I had to find a secret reading place."

"A secret reading place? What's that?" I said.

"Well, it's different for everybody," said Jessie. "But once you find it, you can read forever."

"Can you tell me where your secret reading place is?" I asked Jessie. "Or is it a secret?" I laughed.

"I actually made my own secret reading place," Jessie said. "I brought pillows and blankets into the kitchen and set up a reading fort under the kitchen table."

"That sounds cool," said Robbie.

"It was really cool," said Jessie. "I brought in my favorite books and some snacks, and before I knew it, a whole hour had passed!"

"That's a really good idea," I said. "Hey, Robbie, do you want to come over after school today, and we can find a secret reading place?"

"Sure," said Robbie. "Maybe we can read up in your tree house."

"My tree house? That's boring," I said. "And besides, it's not so secret. Suzie can find us up there. I know a better place."

"You do?" said Robbie. "Where?"

"It wouldn't be a secret if everyone knew about it," I whispered. "If I tell you now, then you know Big-Mouth Bully will announce it to the whole bus."

Max leaned over the seat and got right in my face. "What did you call me?"

I gulped. The kid has supersonic hearing. "I, uh . . . I, uh . . . ," I stammered.

He grabbed my shirt. "I said, what did you call me?"

"He called you Big-Mouth Bully," said Jessie. "Because that's what you are. You are a big bully."

Jessie was so brave. She was the only one brave enough to stand up to Max.

"Let go of his shirt."

Max looked over at Jessie.

"Now," she said.

Max slowly let go of my shirt.

"Thanks," I whispered to Jessie.

"Any time," Jessie said, smiling. "Any time."

"I'll just wait until school is over, and then you can show me the secret place," said Robbie.

I put my finger to my lips, and then I gave Robbie a thumbs-up. "It will just be our little secret," I whispered.

CHAPTER 6

The Secret Reading Place

Robbie and I couldn't wait for school to be over so we could go to my secret reading place.

"You're just going to love it," I said to Robbie as we walked into my house.

"Love what?" said Suzie.

"None of your beeswax," I said.

"She is such a busybody," Robbie whispered to me.

"I know," I whispered back.

"Mom," Suzie called. "Freddy is telling secrets."

"I am not," I said.

"Then why were you just whispering to Robbie?"

"Leave them alone, Suzie," said my mom. "Would you all like something to eat?"

"We are actually going to take our snack outside," I said.

"Why?" said Suzie.

"It's for us to know and you to find out," I said, smiling at Robbie.

"UGGHHH!" groaned Suzie. "Sometimes you are such a pain!" She dropped her backpack and went into the other room.

"Good," I whispered. "Now she won't follow us outside."

"What would you boys like to take out there with you?" my mom asked.

"How about some crackers, a cheese stick, and some juice," I said.

"That sounds good to me," Robbie said, rubbing his stomach. "I love cheese sticks." Just then his stomach grumbled. "That's my stomach saying, 'I like cheese sticks, too,'" Robbie said, laughing.

"I'll just put everything in a little bag," said my mom. "That will make it easier to take outside."

"Thanks, Mom," I said, grabbing the bag. Robbie and I took our books out of our backpacks and headed out the back door.

"So which way do we go?" Robbie asked.

"Follow me," I said, "but be very quiet. I don't want Suzie to hear us."

Robbie gave me a salute. "Aye, aye, Captain," he said.

I started walking toward the back of my yard.

"Oh, I think I know where we're going," said Robbie.

"Really, smarty-pants," I said. "Where?"

"To your big tree," said Robbie. "We'll climb up and sit in the branches to read our books."

"Are you crazy?" I said. "Don't you remember what happened the last time I climbed that tree?"

"Oh yeah," Robbie said, laughing. "You fell out of the tree and broke your arm."

"I'm glad *you* think it's funny," I said. "*I* didn't think it was so funny."

"So, I guess the tree isn't your secret reading place," said Robbie. "It would be kind of hard to hold on to the branch and turn the page at the same time."

We kept walking.

"I thought you said we weren't going to the tree house," said Robbie.

"We're not," I said.

"It looks like we are headed right for it."

"Just hold on," I said. "We're almost there."

We both took a few more steps. "Here we are," I said.

Robbie looked around. "I don't see any secret place," he said. "All I see is this big bush."

I smiled. "That's it."

"What's it?" said Robbie.

"That's it," I said, pointing.

"What are you pointing at?" asked Robbie. "The bush?"

"Yep." I nodded my head.

"Now I really think you are crazy," said Robbie, making the cuckoo sign next to his head.

"I'm not crazy," I said. "This bush is actually hollow. There is a big empty space inside. I like to hide in there when Suzie and I play hide-and-seek. She can never find me."

"Really?" said Robbie.

"Really," I said. "Come on in."

I got down on my hands and knees and crawled into the bush. Robbie followed me.

"Wow! You were right," said Robbie. "It is really cool in here. And it is definitely secret. No one would ever know you were in here."

We sat down on the ground, and I pulled our snack out of the bag.

"Thanks," said Robbie. "I'm starving."

He gobbled his cheese stick and his stomach growled again.

I laughed. "Is that your stomach saying 'thank you'?" I said.

"Yep," Robbie said, patting his tummy.

I nibbled a bit of my crackers and cheese and put the rest back in the bag to save for later. Then I lay down on the ground. I picked up one of my books and started to read.

After a little while, I felt something crawling up my arm. "Hey, look," I said to Robbie.

"What?" he said.

"We have a friend." I held out my arm so Robbie could see the little worm crawling past my elbow.

"He's really cute," said Robbie.

"He tickles," I said.

"Can I feel?" said Robbie.

"Sure," I said. I carefully picked up the worm and put it on Robbie's arm.

Robbie giggled. "You're right," he said. "He does tickle when he crawls."

The worm crawled onto Robbie's book. Robbie laughed.

"What's so funny?" I said.

"I think we have a bookworm," said Robbie

"It looks like he likes to read," I said.

"Let's call him Buddy," said Robbie. "He can be our reading buddy."

"Buddy the Worm. I like that," I said.

We sat hidden in the bush reading with Buddy until we heard my mom calling us. "Freddy, Robbie, time to come in now!"

I gently picked up Buddy and put him in the pocket of my T-shirt. "Come with me, little bookworm," I said. "You can be my reading buddy for the whole week."

Robbie and I both got up and crawled out of the bush.

"Wow! Jessie was right," I said. "If you find a secret reading place, you *can* read forever!"

CHAPTER 7

Buddy

Robbie and I raced into the house.

"Where have you boys been?" my mom asked. "I didn't see you anywhere in the yard. I thought you had magically made yourselves invisible."

"Oh, we were invisible, all right," I said. I turned to Robbie and whispered, "See, I told you that was a great secret place."

"It was so quiet," said my mom. "I didn't hear a sound. What were you doing out there?"

"Reading," we said together.

"Reading? You spent the whole hour out there reading?"

"Were we really out there for an hour?" I said. "It felt like twenty minutes."

"It was sixty minutes," said my mom. "I'm impressed."

Robbie and I gave each other a high five. "That's sixty more minutes we each get to write down on our Read-a-thon page, and two more hours for the whole class!" Robbie said.

"Woohoo!"

"Is your class doing something, too?" asked my mom.

"Oh, Mom, I forgot to tell you that the kid who reads the most gets the five free books, but the class that reads the most wins a visit by a real live author!"

"That's exciting," said my mom. "I don't think you've ever met an author in person."

"I haven't," I said.

"I haven't, either," said Robbie. "If we win, I want to get her autograph."

"Great idea!" I said. "I love getting autographs!"

"Do you know which author would be coming?" my mom asked.

"Nope. Mrs. Wushy told us it's a surprise."

"Well, that's a wonderful surprise. I'm glad you two are so excited about reading."

"How much longer until dinner, Mom?"

"Not for another hour," my mom said. "I'm making your favorite, spaghetti and meatballs."

This time my tummy grumbled. "That's my stomach saying, 'I like spaghetti and meatballs,'" I said to Robbie.

We all laughed.

"While we're waiting, can we do some reading on the computer?" I asked my mom.

"Before you do anything in this house, you two need to wash your hands. You look like you've been digging in the dirt," said my mom.

Right when she said that, I felt Buddy start to move in my pocket. My mom gets freaked out by creepy-crawly things, so I'm not allowed to bring any into the house. My plan was to sneak Buddy up to my room before my mom saw him.

Too late for that plan. I guess when Buddy heard my mom say "dirt," he got excited and poked his little head out of my shirt pocket.

"AAAAAHHHHHHHH!" my mom screamed. "What is that?" she said, pointing to my pocket.

I lifted Buddy out and put him on my finger.

"It's just a little worm. See, Mom?" I said, holding him up so she could get a good look at him.

"No, Freddy, I don't want to see. Get that thing away from me."

I laughed. "It's just a little earthworm. He won't hurt you."

"I know he won't hurt me," said my mom. "I just don't like slimy things that live in the dirt. Please take it back outside right now. You know my rules. No critters in the house."

"Oh, but he's my bookworm. He's my reading buddy," I said. "He's going to keep me company

when I read. Then I can read for lots of minutes and win the Read-a-thon."

"Well, he can keep you company outside. You are not going to keep him in this house," said my mom. "You can keep him in your tree house."

"But, Mom . . ."

"Now, Freddy."

"Oh, okay," I said. "Come on, Robbie. Let's go put Buddy in the tree house."

We walked back outside.

"Wow! Your mom sure got freaked out," said Robbie.

"I know," I said. "I don't know why she's so afraid of this little guy."

"I think he's cute," said Robbie.

"I think so, too," I said. I lifted Buddy up to my face. "Don't listen to my mom, Buddy. Robbie and I think you're super cute."

We climbed up the ladder to my tree house and looked around for my bug jar.

"I think the last time we used it, we were collecting worms to feed to Winger, that baby bird we rescued," said Robbie.

"Yeah, I think you're right," I said. Buddy wriggled around in my hand. I laughed. "Don't worry, little guy. We're not going to feed you to any birds."

"Found it!" Robbie yelled, holding up the bug jar. "It was right behind your box of baseball cards."

"We'd better put some dirt and grass in the bottom of the jar so Buddy has a nice, comfy home," I said.

Robbie took the jar, and I carefully carried Buddy down the ladder.

"Put him down on the ground," said Robbie. "Let's see where he crawls. Then we'll know what kind of stuff he likes."

I put Buddy down in the dirt, and he wiggled over to where the dirt was kind of wet.

"Just what I thought," said Robbie. "He likes to be where it's damp."

"What does that mean?" I said.

"It means he likes his dirt to be a little wet. A little more like mud," said Robbie.

Robbie was an expert on animals. He had so many pets in his house. It was like a zoo over there.

"We should also put some leaves in the jar for him to munch on," said Robbie. "That should keep him happy."

We lined the bottom of Buddy's jar with some mud, grass, and leaves. Then I carefully put Buddy into his new home.

I held the jar up to my face. "Sorry, Buddy," I said, "but you're going to have to stay out in the tree house. You're not allowed in the real house. I think you're cute, but my mom thinks you're yucky."

Robbie and I put Buddy back up in the tree house. "Don't be scared, little bookworm," I said as I turned to leave. "I'll be back to read with you every day."

CHAPTER 8

And the Winner Is . . .

I did read with Buddy in my secret reading place every day for a week. I also read on the bus, in a tent, and even in the bathtub! I had to be really careful in the tub so my book didn't get wet.

Finally, it was the day to count up all our reading minutes and turn them in to the office.

At breakfast, my mom said, "Freddy and Suzie, do you both have your Read-a-thon papers to take to school today?"

"I've got mine right here!" I said, waving my paper in the air.

"Hey, watch it, weirdo," said Suzie. "You almost hit me in the eye with that."

"Sorry," I said. "I'm just really excited. I hope I win the five free books."

"Well, let me get my calculator and add up all your minutes," said my mom. "Good luck."

"He's going to need it," said Suzie. "I just know I read more minutes than Freddy."

"How do *you* know?" I said.

"I just know," Suzie said, grinning.

"As soon as I add these both up, we'll have the answer," said my mom. "I'll do Suzie's first."

My mom punched a bunch of buttons on the calculator. "Wow! Good for you, Suzie. You read for a total of three hundred and sixty minutes! I am very impressed."

"So am I," said my dad. "Excellent work."

I frowned. "I'm never going to beat that," I mumbled to myself.

"Now it's Freddy's turn," said my mom. She punched the buttons again. "Oh my goodness. Will you look at that?"

"What?" said Suzie.

"What?" I said.

"Freddy read for a total of three hundred and ninety minutes," said my mom. "That's thirty more minutes than Suzie."

"Woohoo!" I yelled, and pumped my fist in the air.

"Way to go, Mouse," said my dad. "I'm very proud of you."

"You see?" my mom said. "You are a super reader. You just need to believe in yourself. I told you that you could do it."

"Suzie, do you have something to say to your brother?" said my dad.

"Congratulations, Freddy," Suzie said. "You won fair and square."

"Thanks," I said, smiling ear to ear.

"You two had better get a move on," said my dad. "You don't want to miss the bus. You need to take your totals to school to see who the individual winner is and who the class winner is."

We grabbed our papers and backpacks and ran out of the house to catch the bus. Today was too important. We didn't want to be late.

We had to turn our papers in to the office early in the morning. Mrs. Wushy said we would know the results after lunch.

As soon as lunch was over, my classmates and I raced back to the classroom.

"I can't wait to hear my name called," Chloe said. "I'm sure I read more minutes than anybody else."

"I read a lot of minutes," said Robbie.

"Me, too!" said Jessie.

Max didn't say anything.

"Yesterday when we walked through the book fair to look at the books, I saw so many I liked," said Jessie.

"I know," I said. "If I'm the winner, it's going to be hard to choose just five."

"You don't have to worry about that," said Chloe, "because I'm going to be the winner. My mother told me so."

"Just because your mother says that, doesn't mean it's true," said Max.

"Yes, it is," said Chloe.

"No, it's not," said Max.

Chloe stamped her foot. "Yes, it is. My mother knows everything."

"We just have to wait and see," said Mrs.

Wushy. "Remember, even if someone does not win the individual prize, we can still win the class prize."

"I'm just so excited," said Jessie. "I don't think I can wait any longer."

"I don't think you'll have to," said Robbie. "I think I hear Mr. Pendergast's voice on the sound system right now."

Chloe stood up and put her finger to her lips. "SSSSSHHHHHHHH! If you're not quiet, then I won't be able to hear my name."

Robbie rolled his eyes. "It's always about her," he whispered.

Jessie giggled. "She is such a little princess."

"First, I want to thank all of you boys and girls for participating in our Read-a-thon here at Lincoln Elementary," said our principal, Mr. Pendergast. "I am so impressed with how much reading you all have done during the past week. Everyone here is a super reader."

"Just say my name!" Chloe whined. "Just say my name."

"Now I would like to announce the name of the person who read for the most minutes over the last seven days. This person will get to pick five free books at the book fair. And the winner is . . ."

"Chloe!" yelled Chloe.

"Max Sellars," said Mr. Pendergast.

We all turned and looked at Max. My mouth dropped open. I was shocked.

"Did he just say 'Max'?" I said to Robbie.

Robbie nodded his head.

"I didn't even know Max liked to read," whispered Jessie.

"I guess you learn something new about people every day," Robbie said.

"Who knew that the biggest bully in our whole grade was also one of the best readers?" I said.

"Congratulations, Max," said Mrs. Wushy. "I'm proud of you."

"Yeah, congratulations, Max," I said.

"Congratulations," said Robbie and Jessie.

Chloe just started crying. "That's not fair!" she wailed. "That's not fair!"

"It's very fair," said Mrs. Wushy. "Chloe, you are being a very bad sport. I think there is something you need to say to Max."

Chloe stared at Max for a long time. "Congratulations," she finally said.

Mr. Pendergast's voice came on again. "And now for the winning class. The teacher whose class had the highest total of reading minutes is . . ."

"Mrs. Wushy. Mrs Wushy," we all chanted together.

"Mrs. Wushy," said Mr. Pendergast.

"Woohoo!" we all screamed, and jumped up and down. "We did it! We did it!"

"Nice job, boys and girls," said Mrs. Wushy. "Because of your hard work, we get to meet a real author. You are all my little bookworms!"

Max lay down on his stomach and started wiggling around.

"What are you doing, Max?" said Mrs. Wushy.

"The worm!" said Max.

We all laughed, and then we all joined in.

DEAR READER,

I am a kindergarten and first-grade teacher. Every year we do a Read-a-thon at my school. The students ask their families, friends, and neighbors to donate a penny (or more) for every minute they read.

Once the Read-a-thon is over, we count up all the money we earned by reading and give that money to other children who really need it. For the past few years, we have donated the money to an organization called 52 Kids, which helps pay for children in Uganda to go to school.

If your school is interested in doing a Read-a-thon and donating the money you earn to this organization, you can find out more about 52 Kids by going to their website: 52kids.org.

Hope you had as much fun reading *The Reading Race* as I had writing it.

HAPPY READING!

Freddy's Fun Pages

FREDDY'S SHARK JOURNAL

I thought I would give you a list of my favorite shark books that you can read for your Read-a-thon.

1. *The Best Book of Sharks* by Claire Llewellyn

2. *National Geographic Readers: Sharks!* by Anne Schreiber

3. *Don't Eat the Teacher* by Nick Ward

4. *Shark vs. Train* by Chris Barton and Tom Lichtenheld

5. *Amazing Sharks!* by Sarah L. Thomson

6. *Sharks* by Gail Gibbons

7. *I'm a Shark* by Bob Shea

8. *The Magic School Bus Chapter Book: Great Shark Escape* by Jennifer Johnston

MAKE YOUR OWN BUDDY THE WORM BOOKMARK!

SUPPLIES:

Green craft foam (or green felt, or green paper)
One black pipe cleaner
2 googly eyes
A black marker
Glue and scissors

DIRECTIONS:

1. Using your green craft foam, cut out 5 circles to make the body of your worm. The biggest circle should be about 2 inches across. The other circles should go down in size, so that the smallest circle is about 1 inch across.

2. Glue the circles together in a line. The bottom of one circle is glued to the top of another circle. The biggest circle, which is the

head, should be on top, and the smallest circle should be on the bottom.

3. Twist the black pipe cleaner to make a small pair of glasses, and then glue them onto your worm's face.

4. Glue the two googly eyes inside the open circles of the glasses.

5. Using the black marker, draw a mouth on the worm's face.

6. Write the word READ on your worm's body. One letter goes in each green circle (except the head).

Now you have a reading buddy just like Freddy!

MY SECRET
READING PLACE

Use this space to draw and write about
your secret reading place.

How many books can you read in a month? Keep track!

Title		Date
_____	finished	_____
_____	finished	_____
_____	finished	_____
_____	finished	_____
_____	finished	_____
_____	finished	_____
_____	finished	_____
_____	finished	_____

Have you read all about Freddy?

Don't miss any of Freddy's funny adventures!